Hairy Maclary's Bone

Lynley Dodd

PUFFIN

Down in the town
by the butcher's shop door,
sat Hairy Maclary
from Donaldson's Dairy.

Out of the door
came Samuel Stone.
He gave Hairy Maclary
his tastiest
bone.

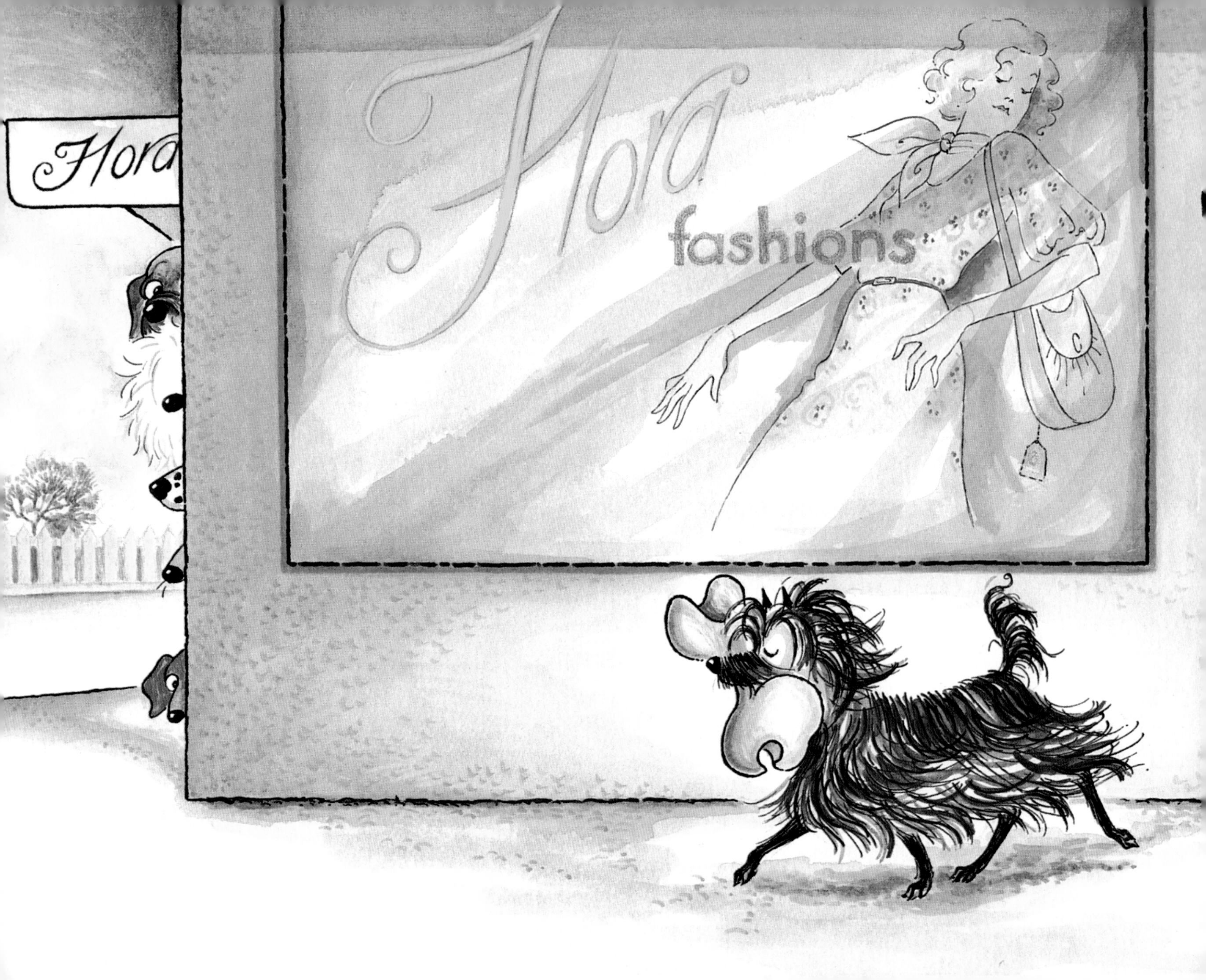
Flora
Flora
fashions

Then off up the street
on scurrying feet,
on his way to the dairy
went Hairy Maclary.

And chasing him home,
with their eyes on the bone,
went Hercules Morse,
Bottomley Potts,
Muffin McLay,
Bitzer Maloney
and Schnitzel von Krumm
with the very low tum.

Hungrily sniffing
and licking their chops,
they followed him up
past the school and the shops.

They came to the sign
selling Sutherland's Sauce.
Through they all went —

except Hercules Morse.

They came to a hedge
along Waterloo Way.
Under they went —

except Muffin McLay.

They came to a yard
full of dinghies and yachts.
Round they all went —

except Bottomley Potts.

They came to a building site,
cluttered and stony.
Over they went —

except Bitzer Maloney.

They came to a wall
by the house of Miss Plum.
One of them jumped —

but not Schnitzel von Krumm.

So at last he was free
to go home on his own,
Hairy Maclary
with ALL of his
bone.

PUFFIN BOOKS
Published by the Penguin Group: London, New York, Australia, Canada, India, Ireland, New Zealand and South Africa
Penguin Books Ltd, Registered Offices: 80 Strand, London WC2R 0RL, England

puffinbooks.com

First published in New Zealand by Mallinson Rendel Publishers Ltd 1984. First published in Great Britain in Puffin Books 1986
069
ISBN: 978-0-140-50558-0